Does God See The Wind?
by Anne de Graaf
Illustrated by Evelyn Rivet

Published by Scandinavia Publishing House
Nørregade 32, DK-1165, Copenhagen K
Denmark

Printed in Italy 1996

Published in the United States of America by
Abingdon Press
201 Eighth Avenue South
Nashville, Tennessee 37203

First Abingdon Press Edition 1996
ISBN 0-687-07149-6

TINY TRIUMPHS

DOES GOD SEE THE WIND?

By Anne de Graaf
Illustrated by Evelyn Rivet

Dedicated to Erik

Abingdon Press

One windy day Julia and her friend Lisa were playing house.

"He is too!"
"He is not!"
"Is too!"
"Is not!"

Julia scrunched up her face.
Lisa stuck out her tongue.
Daniel did, too.

Daddy looked up from the car.
"Children, why are you fighting?"

"I'm the mother and Lisa's the father and she won't pray before we eat."
"My mommy says you don't have to pray."
"Yes, you do!"
"She stuck her tongue out!"

Daddy wiped the grease off his hands.
"All right. This is not something to fight about. Let's have lunch."

But at lunch, Mommy prayed.
When she finished Daniel said,
"Lisa kept her eyes open!"
"How could you tell?"
"My eyes were open."

Daddy said, "That's enough. Lisa is our guest. Daniel and Julia, you be nice now. Lisa can do whatever she's used to doing at home."

Later that day, Lisa went home.
Then Mommy took the children for a walk in the park.
"Why do we pray?" Julia asked.
"Why do you ask?"
"Because Lisa says God isn't real!"

That's when Mommy asked God for the right words.
After a moment she said,
"Have you heard the trees talking to you?"
Daniel stopped.
Julia smiled. "It's the wind!"

Mommy laughed.
"Yes. Can you see the wind?"
Daniel looked high and made his eyes small. He wanted to see the wind, but couldn't.

"Can you see what the wind does?"
"Yes!"
Each child gathered an armful of leaves and threw them up high.
"This is what the wind does!"

Mommy took their hands in hers.
"Now listen closely. The wind is like God.
We can't see Him, but we can see all that He does for us."

"That's why we pray?"
Julia asked.
"Yes, to thank God for all He does,
like giving us
enough to eat."

Daniel squinted.
He still wanted to see the wind.

Then Mommy said, "Close your eyes. Can you feel the wind?"
"Yes!"

Both children spread their arms out and ran around in circles.
"This is how the wind feels!"
Mommy hugged them close.
"Now who knows where God lives?"
"In our hearts!"
"Yes, and that's where we can feel Him. If we close our eyes when we pray, it's easier to feel Him in our hearts."

Daniel closed his eyes and poked his tummy.

"I can feel Him! I can feel God! He's hard and long and. . . ."

"That's your rib!"

"Here, let me feel!"

"Me, too!"

"Oh no!"

Julia and Mommy tickled Daniel.

That's when Mommy thanked God for His right words.

The next day Daddy worked some more on the car.
Lisa and Julia were outside playing.

"He does too!"
"He does not!"
"Does too!"
"Does not!"

Julia put her hands on her hips.
"God does things, just like the wind.
You think the wind is real, don't you?"
Lisa said, "Yes."
"Well then, if you believe in the wind, you can believe in God."

Lisa looked at her shoe.
She asked, "Do you want to play house?"
Julia nodded and the girls ran inside.

Daniel looked high and made his eyes small.
Then he crawled under the car.
"Daddy," he asked, "does God see the wind?"